TALKIN' FOOTBALL

BY JIM GIGLIOTTI · ILLUSTRATED BY JAMES HORVATH

Published by The Child's World®
1980 Lookout Drive • Mankato, MN 56003-1705
800-599-READ • www.childsworld.com

Photos ©: Cover: Eugene Onischenko/Shutterstock. Interior: AP Images: M. Sprecher 16; Scott Boehm 19. Newscom: Rich Graessle/Icon SW 5; Kamil Krzaczynski/UPI 13; Ian Halperin/UPI 17; John Korduner/Icon SW 20. Joe Robbins: 4, 7, 10, 12, 15, 21. Shutterstock: Mtsariaide 6B; Dotshock 6T; lightspring 8; Stan Fino 9; Stephen McSweeny 11; Herbert Kratky. US Air Force: Sr. Airman Ned T. Johnston 1.

Copyright © 2020 by The Child's World®
All rights reserved. No part of this book may be reproduced or utilized in any form or by any means without written permission from the publisher.

ISBN 9781503835726
LCCN 2019943130

Printed in the United States of America

TABLE OF CONTENTS

Introduction . . . 4
Gear Up . . . 6
On the Field . . . 8
Playing the Game . . . 10
Stat City . . . 14
Football People . . . 16
Fun Stuff . . . 18
Heard on TV . . . 20

Glossary . . . 22
Find Out More . . . 23
Index and About the Author and Illustrator . . . 24

INTRODUCTION

"The tall field general stood in the pocket and avoided a sack. Then he threw a bomb deep into the red zone!" If you don't "talk" football, that sentence makes no sense. This book is here to help!

Every sport has its own language. The sport's words and phrases mean something to any real fan. The more of those words you can learn, the more you'll enjoy every game you watch. In this book, we'll explore football. Ready, set . . . hike!

I can't bounce as high as a Super Ball. But when I hit the ground, I bounce in weird directions. It can be funny watching a player try to pick me up!

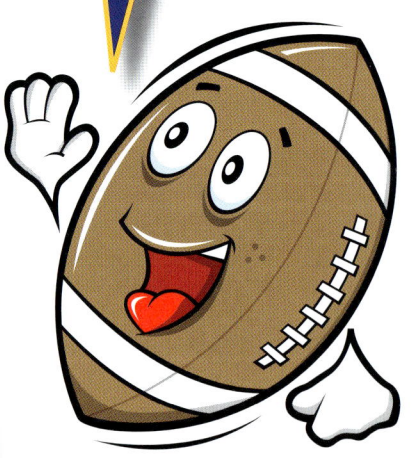

◂ The player with the ball is about to hike it. Teams meet at the line of scrimmage. (See page 10.)

The Name of the Game

In the rest of the world, football is the sport that Americans call soccer. In the US, though, it's the sport that started out as part soccer and part rugby. Despite the name, most of the points in American football are scored by running and passing the ball, not kicking it!

▼ *The Super Bowl trophy is named for the famous coach Vince Lombardi.*

Super Bowl

The championship game of the National Football League (NFL) is called the Super Bowl. The idea for the name came when one NFL team owner saw his kids playing with a Super Ball. That's a small, rubber ball that bounces super high!

Gear Up

Football can be rough. Players wear gear for protection. Each player wears a helmet, pads, gloves, and more. A football player looks like a gladiator ready for battle.

The Ball

"Pigskin" is the most common nickname for the football. However, footballs were never made from pigs! The outside of the ball is made with leather.

▲ *Each player wears a jersey with a number, along with a helmet on his or her head.*

The Helmet

In the early days of football, not everyone wore helmets. The first helmets were soft leather. The players folded them up and put them in their pocket after the game! Today's helmets are made of hard plastic. They have lots of padding for protection.

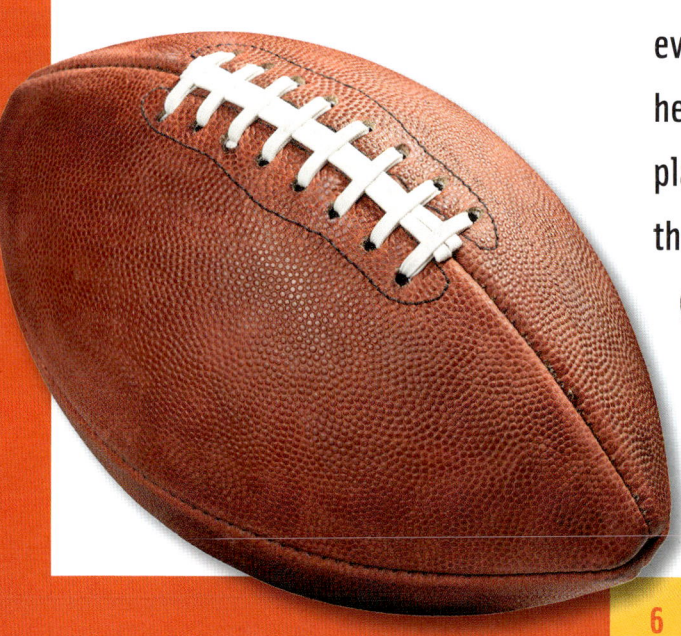

Pads

Shoulder pads, hip pads, thigh pads . . . a football player is well padded! Today's pads are designed to spread the force of a big hit. Being hit still hurts . . . just not as much.

▲ *Check out the thigh and knee pads on this NFL player.*

Am I a college football or an NFL football? Look for the stripes! The college ball has white stripes painted near each end. The NFL ball does not.

Coaches

Football coaches don't wear uniforms. They can make their own fashion statement. Hall of Famer Tom Landry always wore a fedora, a type of hat. "Dapper Dan" Reeves often wore a suit and tie. Patriots coach Bill Belichick is more casual. He usually wears a hoodie.

ON THE FIELD

You know that a football field has yard lines painted from sideline to sideline. But did you know that in the early days of the sport, lines were painted from end zone to end zone, too? That made a big pattern of squares. From up in the stands, it looked like a metal grill called a gridiron. Gridirons were used to cook meat or fish over a fire. Ever since, a football field has been called a gridiron.

The Goal Post

Gold-painted pipes rise high above the back of each end zone. Successful kicks must go between them. The pipes are 35 feet (10.7 km) tall and 18.5 feet (5.6 m) apart. The crossbar between them is 10 feet (3 m) off the ground. Together, the uprights, the crossbar, and the post that holds them in place are called the goal post.

Pylons

The receiver catches the ball and heads for the end zone. He dives toward the pylon! Did he make it in? Pylons are the small orange cones at the four corners of the end zone. They are actually in the end zone. If a player with the ball touches one, it's a touchdown!

► So Many Lines

A football field is 100 yards (91.4 m) long. Lines mark off each yard. Painted numbers help fans keep track of the yard lines. The small marks in the middle are called hashmarks. Each new play starts on or near one of them.

◄ Go for Six!

If a team carries the ball into the 10-yard (9.1-m) end zone, it gets a touchdown and six points.

◄ The Red Zone

When a team that has the ball crosses the opponent's 20-yard line, it has moved into this area of the field.

PLAYING THE GAME

The running back grabs the rock and breaks it all the way to the house! Translation: The runner takes the football and races all the way to the end zone. It's a touchdown! Let's explore some other words you hear during football action.

Line of Scrimmage
This line is not painted on the field. It is the line where each play starts. The two teams line up on each side of this line. Then the offense runs a play. After the play is over, a new line of scrimmage is set.

The QB
From the Shotgun, the rifle-armed signal caller drops back to pass! The Shotgun is a name for how the quarterback often lines up. The quarterback (QB) is the signal caller. He's the man who makes a team's offense go. He is a great passer and a top leader.

Time for Pancakes!

The offensive lineman pancakes the defender, allowing the running back to take it to the next level! When a lineman pancakes a player, it means he flattened him onto his back. A running back who breaks through the defensive line gets to the next level, which includes the linebackers. If he gets through that level, he's into the secondary—and off to the races!

▼ Receivers wear sticky gloves to help them make diving catches.

Almost every play starts when the quarterback yells "Hut!" Why "hut"? Some people think it came from the military. In the army, they'll say "Ten-hut!" when they mean "Attention!"

Great Hands!

That's what fans say about a player who catches the ball a lot. Quarterbacks pass the ball to their teammates. The receivers leap and dive to catch the ball. Great pass plays are often big **highlights**!

11

◄ The Rams' Aaron Donald sacks Green Bay star Aaron Rodgers.

Oops! Looks like this QB's blockers left a gap and a "sackmaster" got through!

Sack Time

The linebacker shoots the gap and drops the quarterback for a big sack! A gap is the space between the linemen who protect the QB. A defensive player can shoot or sprint through the gap. When he tackles the quarterback before a pass, it's called a sack.

Scramble!

Sometimes a QB can't make a pass. He might have to run. That's called a "scramble." Some quarterbacks are great runners and can gain key yards for their team on their feet!

Nickels and Dimes

The nickel back jumps the route to intercept a pass and post a pick-six! A nickel back is an extra defensive back. Teams bring him in when they expect a pass. If a team brings in two extra defensive backs, the second one is a dime back. Why? Because two nickels equal a dime! A pick-six is an **interception** that is returned for a touchdown.

▶ *Great D! No. 23 is a defensive back. He has stripped the ball from No. 17's hands.*

Touchdown Dance

Whether the offense or defense scores a touchdown, it's time for a party. Many teams put on a mini-show in the end zone. They dance, pose, and high-five. Getting to the end zone is hard work. The players enjoy a chance to celebrate!

STAT CITY

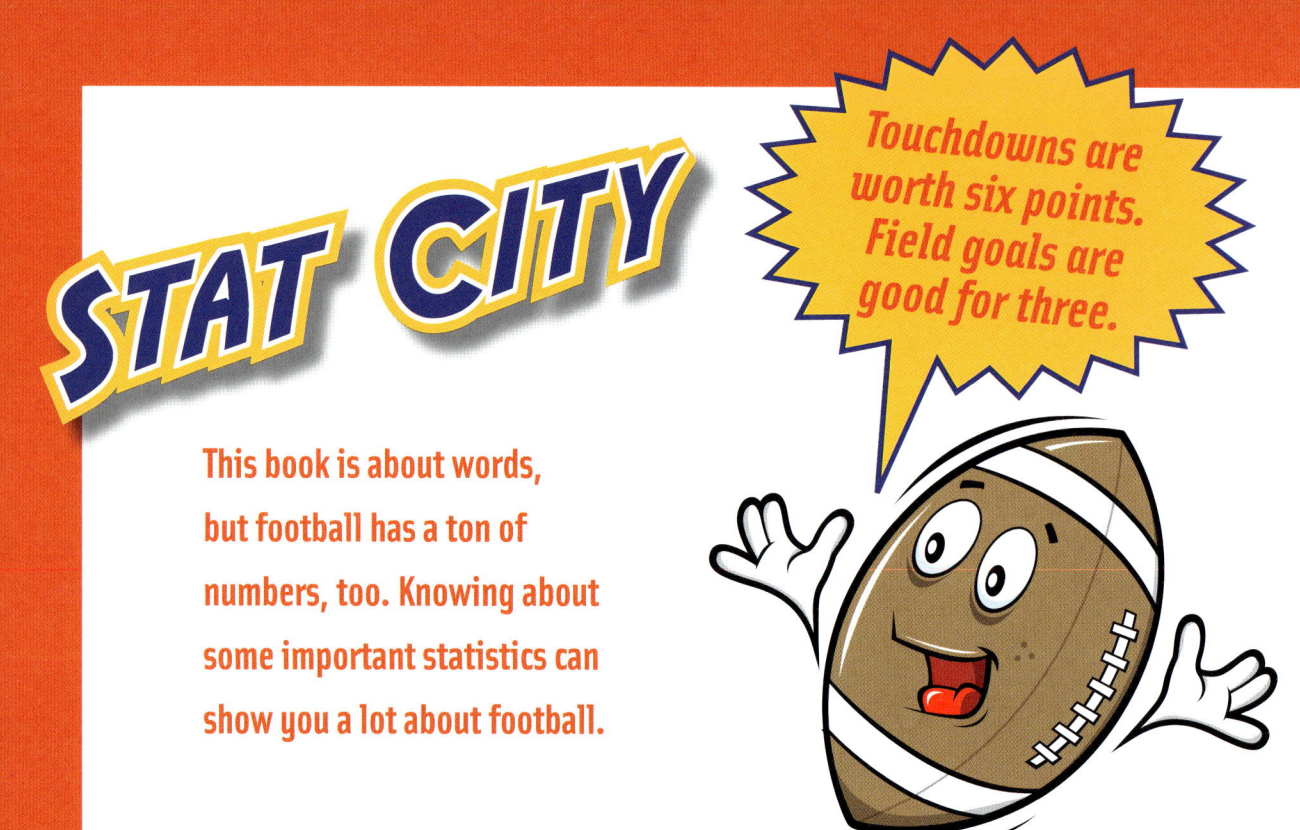

Touchdowns are worth six points. Field goals are good for three.

This book is about words, but football has a ton of numbers, too. Knowing about some important statistics can show you a lot about football.

Doing Math

Completion Percentage: This measures how often a quarterback completes a pass. That is, he throws it and a receiver catches it. In 2018, New Orleans Saints quarterback Drew Brees set an NFL record. He completed 74.4 percent of his passes. That's just about three out of every four!

Yards Per Carry: This measures the average number of yards that a player gains on a running play. Anything over 4.0 is good; over 5.0 is excellent!

Combined Net Yards: This is a total of all the yards that a player gains. The yards come from catching passes and running. Add in yards gained returning kicks. This stat reveals the best all-around players.

Numbers Game

Did you know you can guess what position someone plays by the uniform number on his back? Here's a chart*:

1 to 19: QBs, punters, kickers, receivers
20-39: Running backs, defensive backs
40-49: Running backs, defensive backs, linebackers, tight ends
50-59: Linebackers, defensive linemen, centers
60-79: Offensive and defensive linemen
80-89: Receivers and tight ends
90-99: Linebackers, defensive linemen

*This works for the NFL only. Also, some players are allowed to have numbers different than their positions.

Counting Stats

Other football stats are easier to figure. Just count! Quarterbacks keep track mostly of passing yards and touchdown passes. Interceptions is a category for them to avoid! Running backs count yards from running and catching passes. Receivers count their number of catches and yards. Everybody keeps track of touchdowns scored! Defenses count tackles and interceptions. They also keep track of sacks and **fumbles**.

▼ *Teams gather in the huddle before most plays.*

15

FOOTBALL PEOPLE

Players, coaches, officials, and fans all pack into the stadium for every game. Some of these football people have fun nicknames.

Officials? They look like zebras! That's a nickname for the folks who enforce the rules!

▶ *This referee is picking up his flag after calling a penalty. Game officials have uniform numbers just like players.*

The Officials

Who are the people in black-and-white shirts? These are the officials, who make sure everyone follows the rules. When the players don't, an official throws a penalty flag. It's a yellow piece of cloth weighted down with sand or beans. The head official is the referee. He is easy to spot. He's the one who wears a white cap.

16

The 12th Man

Each college and pro team has 11 players on the field. So how can there be a 12th man? That's a nickname for football fans. Hometown crowds cheer loudly for their team! In Seattle, the Seahawks love their 12th man a lot. They have retired the jersey No. 12. No Seattle player will ever wear that uniform number again.

Who Are Mike, Sam, and Will?

Many NFL teams have linebackers called Mike, Sam, and Will. How can so many players have the same name? Because those aren't their real names! They stand for the linebacker positions. Mike is for the middle, Sam is for the strong side, and Will is for the weak side. The strong side is where the offense has an extra player (the tight end) on the line.

◄ *NFL fans love to dress up. This Seattle fans celebrates his team's No. 12 tradition.*

FUN STUFF

American football was first played in 1869. Since then, fans and players have come up with some great slang words and terms. Here are some every fan should know.

audible
When a quarterback changes the play at the line of scrimmage. He uses hand signals or voice signals.

bump-and-run
A way of covering a receiver. The defensive player bumps him when the play starts, then runs with him.

chip shot
This term that has been borrowed from golf. In football, it means a short field-goal try.

▲ *This kicker is booting a chip shot to get three points for his team.*

Passing Fancy
Football has more passing today than ever before. Here are some key passing terms. A long pass is a "bomb." A long pass at the end of a game that a team is losing is called a "Hail Mary." The quarterback throws the ball as far as he can! Good quarterbacks throw perfect spirals. That means the ball is thrown with no wobble at all!

18

hang time

The time that a punt is in the air before it is caught.

special teams

The players who are on the field for a kickoff, a punt, a field-goal try, or an extra-point try.

This is every player's favorite play. It means their team is about to win!

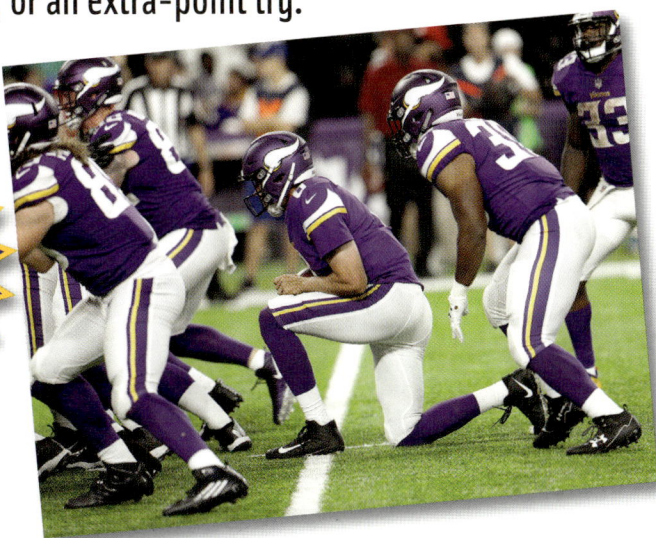

two-minute drill

Sometimes called a "Hurry-Up Offense," it is used when a team needs to run plays quickly and score fast.

victory formation

The team with the ball has the lead. Just a few seconds are left. In this lineup, the QB just kneels down to end the play. No chance of a fumble!

Heard on TV

Watch any football game on TV or sit in the stands and you'll hear words that sound like a whole new language. Here are a few of our favorites.

blind side

In the direction of the quarterback's back. He can't see a defensive player that is coming from that side.

blitz

This means the quarterback had better watch out! It's when a defense expects a pass and sends extra rushers.

goal-line stand

When a defense prevents the offense from scoring from very close to the goal line.

Oof! Grunt! Erg! C'mon, guys, we gotta make this goal-line stand!

icing the kicker

When a kicker lines up for a key field-goal try, some opposing teams like to call time out. They want to make the kicker worry. Sometimes it works. Sometimes it doesn't!

RPO

It means "run-pass option." The QB chooses to run or pass after the play begins.

scramble

Quarterbacks who are in danger of getting sacked run around. They try not to get sacked!

stunt

Defensive players try to trick the offensive blockers. They twist around each other instead of running straight ahead.

▲ Even the great Tom Brady has to scramble sometimes!

Great Player Nicknames

You don't need to have a great nickname to make it to the Hall of Fame . . . but it can't hurt! Here are a few of the best players in NFL history with the best nicknames.

"Slingin' Sammy" Baugh

Tom "The Goat" Brady (that means G.O.A.T., or Greatest of All Time)

"Mean Joe" Greene

Ted "The Mad Stork" Hendricks

Elroy "Crazylegs" Hirsch

Deion "Prime Time" Sanders

GLOSSARY

enforce (en-FORSE) make someone follow the rules of a game

fumble (FUM-bull) a ball that is dropped by a player who is carrying it

gladiator (GLAD-ee-ay-ter) from ancient Rome, a fighter who performs for fans

Hall of Famer (HALL UV FAY-mer) a person who is honored as a member of the Pro Football Hall of Fame, located in Canton, Ohio

highlights (HY-lytz) in sports, short video clips of the most important or memorable moments during a game

interception (in-ter-SEPP-shun) a pass that is caught by the defense instead of the offense that threw it

penalty (PEN-ul-tee) when a player breaks one of football's rules during a game

percentage (per-SENN-tij) a measurement of how often something happens

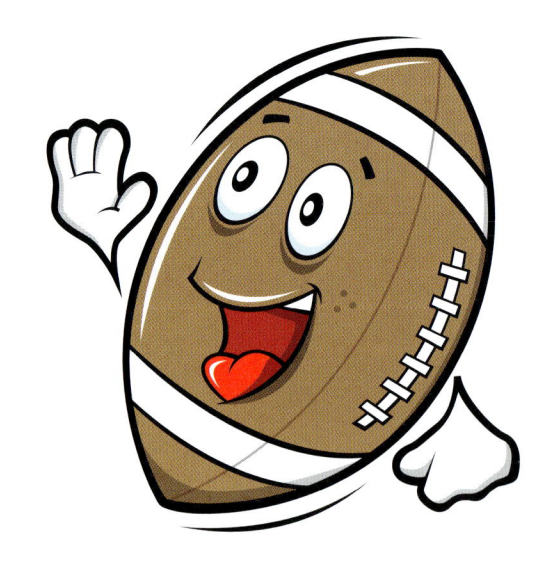

FIND OUT MORE

IN THE LIBRARY

Gramling, Gary. *The Football Fanbook: Everything You Need to Become a Gridiron Know-It-All.* New York, NY: Time Inc. Books, 2017.

Jacobs, Greg. *The Everything Kids' Football Book (6th Edition).* Avon, MA: Adams Media, 2018.

Levit, Joe. *Football's G.O.A.T: Jim Brown, Tom Brady, and More!* Minneapolis, MN: Lerner Books, 2019.

ON THE WEB

Visit our Web site for links about football:

childsworld.com/links

Note to Parents, Teachers, and Librarians: We routinely verify our Web links to make sure they are safe and active sites. So encourage your readers to check them out!

INDEX

12th man, 17
Baugh, "Slingin'" Sammy, 21
Belichick, Bill, 7
Brady, Tom, 21
defense, 13, 15, 20
Donald, Aaron, 12
field diagram, 9
football, name of sport, 5
gear, 6, 7
Greene, "Mean" Joe, 21
Hendricks, Ted "The Mad Stork," 21
Hirsch, Elroy "Crazylegs," 21
history, 5, 18, 21

Landry, Tom, 7
Mike, Sam, and Will, 17
offense, 10, 11, 13, 17, 18, 19, 20
officials, 16
quarterbacks, 10, 11, 12, 14, 15, 18, 19
Reeves, "Dapper Dan," 7
Rodgers, Aaron, 12
Sanders, Deion "Prime Time," 21
Seattle Seahawks, 17
statistics, 14
Super Bowl, 5
uniform numbers, 15

About the Author and Illustrator

Jim Gigliotti is the author of more than 50 books for young readers, including many biographies and lots of sports books! He lives near Los Angeles, CA. James Horvath is an illustrator and cartoonist based in California. He has written and illustrated several children's books, including Dig, Dogs, Dig! *and* Build, Dogs, Build!